ACKNOWLEDGMENTS

This story is inspired by the real life of the Parent family. Ken and Rachel (my son-in-law and my daughter) have lived this example of love and have seen so many lives transformed through their loving sacrifices.

Thank you to my beautiful wife, Ronna, through whom flows so much kindess and love. Her servant's heart inspires us all.

Special thanks to Janice Buswell for her amazing ability to give my words a bear/child's voice.

GROUCHY BEAR

Finds a Family

Written by
Tim Walterbach

Illustrated by
Elizabeth Walterbach

Grouchy Bear lived alone. He was very, very lonely. He'd lost his mother and father. Actually, it was worse than that. His mother and father had forgotten him.

Grouchy Bear's parents LOVED honey. They loved honey so much that they started hunting for it every day. Each time they left, they stayed away longer and longer. They forgot how much Grouchy Bear needed them.

I'm so hungry...

One day, they never came home.

Grouchy Bear was sad, afraid, and very, very lonely. There was no one to help!

Because he was so sad and lonely and afraid, Grouchy Bear began to...

...sleep too long...

...eat too much honey...

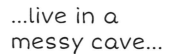

...live in a messy cave...

Sometimes, he couldn't sleep at all. On top of all that, Grouchy Bear started growling.

Grouchy felt so sad every time he saw the other kids with their happy families. He wanted to be happy, too. Instead, he got grouchier and grouchier. But it was worst at this time of year: Christmastime. Grouchy Bear hated seeing other kids enjoy Christmas.
It just wasn't fair.

Most of all, he hated to spend
Christmas all alone.

At first, Grouchy Bear had hope. Other families felt sorry for Grouchy and let him stay with them. They let him sleep in their house and eat their food. But it seemed like they loved their own kids more than they loved Grouchy.

Which only made Grouchy feel sadder.

Worse, the other kids teased him for not having a family. They made fun of him for his grouchy ways and bad habits. Grouchy Bear grew grouchier and grouchier and sadder and sadder.

And as he got grouchier, he slept even later, ate more honey, made more messes, and growled even more.

And no matter where Grouchy Bear went, something always went wrong. And guess who got blamed?

Sometimes he even roared.

Grouchy did.

The last house had been the worst.

One day, the parents said he was making life too hard. He would have to go back to his cave until he could behave better.

What was he going to do?

That night, Grouchy Bear looked into the sky and prayed for a family that would truly love him for who he is. No matter what. He hoped that, when he woke up, his parents would be home.

The next morning he woke up all alone.

That day was his angriest day of all.

Grouchy stormed out of his cave,
looking for someone to scare. The
first people he saw were five children
picking flowers and playing together.

They looked so happy. It only made
him angrier. He wanted them to feel
as scared as he did. So he ran at
them with his scariest growl!

But to his surprise...

...they turned and gave him...
a bouquet of flowers!

RAWR!

"I'm Petunia!" one said. "And I'm Plucky! And the little ones are Khan, Kubla, and Cannonball," the other added with a wide smile.

Before Grouchy Bear could answer, the little girls yelled, "Knuckle, Chuckle, Garfunkel, come here!!!"

Suddenly, three little boys appeared, laughing and playing around. They took one look at Grouchy Bear and asked him a very serious question:

"Hey, you want to come play?"

Grouchy Bear was SO surprised. He forgot to be angry. Instead, he played and played and played with his new friends.

When they finally stopped playing, Grouchy told them a little about his life.

To his surprise, Chuckle said, "We lost our families, too, but now we have another family, and they love us SO much! We have to go eat dinner now. See you later, Grouchy Bear!"

Grouchy watched as the boys left.

Sadly, Grouchy Bear turned away, heading back to his own lonely cave. And as he did, he was grouchier than ever.

He still had no family. No love. Not even dinner.

He almost wished he'd never met those kids at all.

Petunia, Kubla, Chuckle, Knuckle, and Garfunkel hurried home to tell Mama and Papa about their new friend and how sad he was. But they had a plan to help.

"We know just what Grouchy needs!" Chuckle said.

"He needs a family he can stay with. One that really loves him!" Petunia said seriously.

Papa looked at them just as seriously. "Some say Grouchy Bear is known for being mean. It would be a lot of work. It could even be dangerous."

"Do you mean he can't live with us?" Petunia asked pitifully.

"I will give him my bed!" offered Garfunkel.

Papa looked at Mama. He could tell Mama wanted Grouchy Bear to live with them even more than the kids did.

She knew that everyone needs love, and they had a lot of love to give.

"I'll tell you what," Papa said. "Let your mama and I talk about it tonight, and we will let you know in the morning."

So Petunia, Chuckle, Knuckle, Kubla, and Garfunkel all went to bed, hoping that in the morning their parents would say "yes!"

Late into the night, Mama, Papa, and the two oldest girls, Twinkle and Periwinkle, came up with a plan.

The next morning, Papa said, "Your mama and I have talked, and we think that Grouchy Bear is so grouchy because he's scared."

"So we just need to tell him that he doesn't need to be scared anymore, right?" Petunia asked.

"And then he can come live with us!" Knuckle added.

Papa shook his head. "It's going to take some time and lots of love to show him that he doesn't need to be afraid..."

The kids' hearts sank. But then Papa smiled. "...so we've made a plan. Is everyone in?"

The kids all cheered!!!

And immediately, Papa began sharing the plan...

Late that morning, Grouchy Bear finally woke up and wandered out of his cave. He was expecting another sad, grouchy, hungry day. But he didn't get far before he ran into Petunia and Plucky. Immediately, he gave his angriest roar. But to his surprise, they had cookies shaped like three men. "We made these for you!" Plucky said excitedly.

Grouchy Bear could hardly believe it. "For me?" He took a big bite. It was delicious.

"Yes! It was Mama's idea!" Petunia grinned. "These are the three wise men. She said to remind you that everyone who is wise seeks Jesus."

Grouchy Bear wasn't sure about that, but as Petunia and Plucky left with a friendly wave, he couldn't help but feel a little less angry than before.

Petunia and Plucky had been so kind that he started to wonder.

Was there really someone who loved him, even as grouchy as he was? No matter what?

The next day, when Grouchy Bear ventured out of his cave, Chuckle, Knuckle, and Garfunkel met him. They were carrying a wooden manger.

"Hi!" Chuckle said, "Our Dad helped us make this to remind us of Jesus, who was born in a manger just like this, and who loves us. No matter what! We want you to have it."

Grouchy Bear took one look at the manger and laughed.

"What kind of bed is that for a baby?"

Knuckle laughed. "There was no other place for him to go!"

Grouchy Bear paused and looked again. "Did your Dad really help you make this?"

"Yes," Garfunkel said earnestly. "Just like Jesus' father worked with him. Our dad likes to spend time with us, too."

As the boys left, Grouchy Bear wondered about this family who was so nice to him. Who was this Jesus fellow they kept talking about?

Is he still a baby or is he grown up now? Is Jesus their neighbor? Or a relative?

"Or is Jesus a kid like me?"

Grouchy Bear
wanted to meet him.

The next day, there was a big KNOCK on Grouchy Bear's door. Outside, Petunia, Chuckle, Knuckle, Garfunkel, Kubla, Twinkle, Periwinkle, and their MOM and DAD stood smiling in at him! Quickly, he opened the door.

"Did you bring Jesus?" he asked.

"Oh no." Mama smiled sweetly. "Jesus lived a long time ago and lives in heaven now, but we will tell you all about him!"

Sitting down beside Grouchy Bear, Papa told the story.

"Jesus loves you. In fact, He loves everyone. When we are mean, He forgives us. He even forgave those who put him on a cross to die.

"But God brought Jesus back to life, so that if you believe in Him and ask Him to forgive you for your grouchy ways, He will give you a joyful heart instead!

"Because He lives forever in Heaven, you can too."

Grouchy Bear was amazed that someone would love him enough to want to be with him forever. "Does Jesus have a family?" he asked.

"Yes! We are part of His family!" Mama said.

"Can I be in it, too?" he asked.

"Of course!" Mama said. Kneeling together, they prayed with Grouchy Bear to become part of Jesus' family.

When they stood up, Grouchy Bear asked, "Is that all? Now am I part of Jesus' family?"

"Yes, you are!" Mama said with a beaming smile. "But that's not all..."

"No?" Grouchy Bear asked, suddenly suspicious. He wondered if it might be a trick.

"No," Papa added with a wink. "We'd love for you to come spend Christmas with us! And if you like it, we hope you'll decide to be a part of our family."

Grouchy Bear was so surprised, he couldn't say a word as Mama and Papa hugged him goodbye.

That night, Grouchy Bear could hardly sleep.

All night long, he thought about the good news. He was part of a new family! He'd been forgiven of everything he'd done wrong! He could start all over! He would live forever with Jesus and his new friends.

The more Grouchy Bear thought about it, the more joyful and loved he felt. And suddenly he knew—he wanted to live with this family!

As the sun came up, Grouchy Bear got an idea. This family had been so nice to him that he wanted to do something nice back.

He remembered in happier times, how his father used to dress up in a Christmas outfit and tell the Christmas story.

So Grouchy dug around in the closet until he found the old Christmas suit and an old Bible with the Christmas story marked in it.

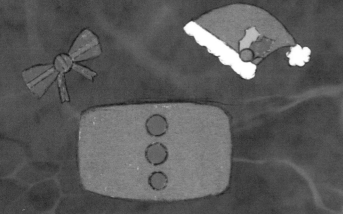

Luke 2

On Christmas Day, he showed up on the doorstep as "Timmy" the Christmas Bear. When Plucky, Petunia, Chuckle, Knuckle, Garfunkel, Kubla, Khan, Cannonball, Twinkle, Periwinkle, Mama, and Papa ALL opened the door, he stepped in and proudly read the story.

"The Birth of Jesus Christ" (Luke 2:1-20)

1 In those days a decree went out from Caesar Augustus that all the world should be registered. 2 This was the first registration when Quirinius was governor of Syria. 3 And all went to be registered, each to his own town.

4 And Joseph also went up from Galilee, from the town of Nazareth, to Judea, to the city of David, which is called Bethlehem, because he was of the house and lineage of David, 5 to be registered with Mary, his betrothed, who was with child. 6 And while they were there, the time came for her to give birth. 7 And she gave birth to her firstborn son and wrapped him in swaddling cloths and laid him in a manger, because there was no place for them in the inn.

8 And in the same region there were shepherds out in the field, keeping watch over their flock by night. 9 And an angel of the Lord appeared to them, and the glory of the Lord shone around them, and they were filled with great fear.

10 And the angel said to them, "Fear not, for behold, I bring you good news of great joy that will be for all the people. 11 For unto you is born this day in the city of David a Savior, who is Christ the Lord. 12 And this will be a sign for you: you will find a baby wrapped in swaddling cloths and lying in a manger."

13 And suddenly there was with the angel a multitude of the heavenly host praising God and saying, 14 "Glory to God in the highest, and on earth peace among those with whom he is pleased!"

15 When the angels went away from them into heaven, the shepherds said to one another, "Let us go over to Bethlehem and see this thing that has happened, which the Lord has made known to us."

16 And they went with haste and found Mary and Joseph, and the baby lying in a manger. 17 And when they saw it, they made known the saying that had been told them concerning this child. 18 And all who heard it wondered at what the shepherds told them.

19 But Mary treasured up all these things, pondering them in her heart. 20 And the shepherds returned, glorifying and praising God for all they had heard and seen, as it had been told them.

Mama and Papa and all the children cheered as they invited him to join their celebration. That Christmas was the best Christmas Grouchy Bear had ever had, full of joy and love and SO many gifts! And somehow Grouchy Bear (who really wasn't very grouchy anymore) knew it definitely wouldn't be his last.

The End.

Printed in the USA
CPSIA information can be obtained
at www.ICGtesting.com
LVRC082053141123
763626LV00001B/1